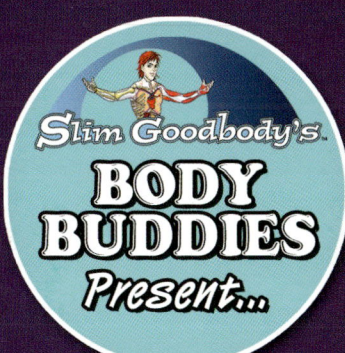

# Slim Goodbody's BODY BUDDIES Present...

# THE REMARKABLE RESPIRATORY SYSTEM

### How do my lungs work?

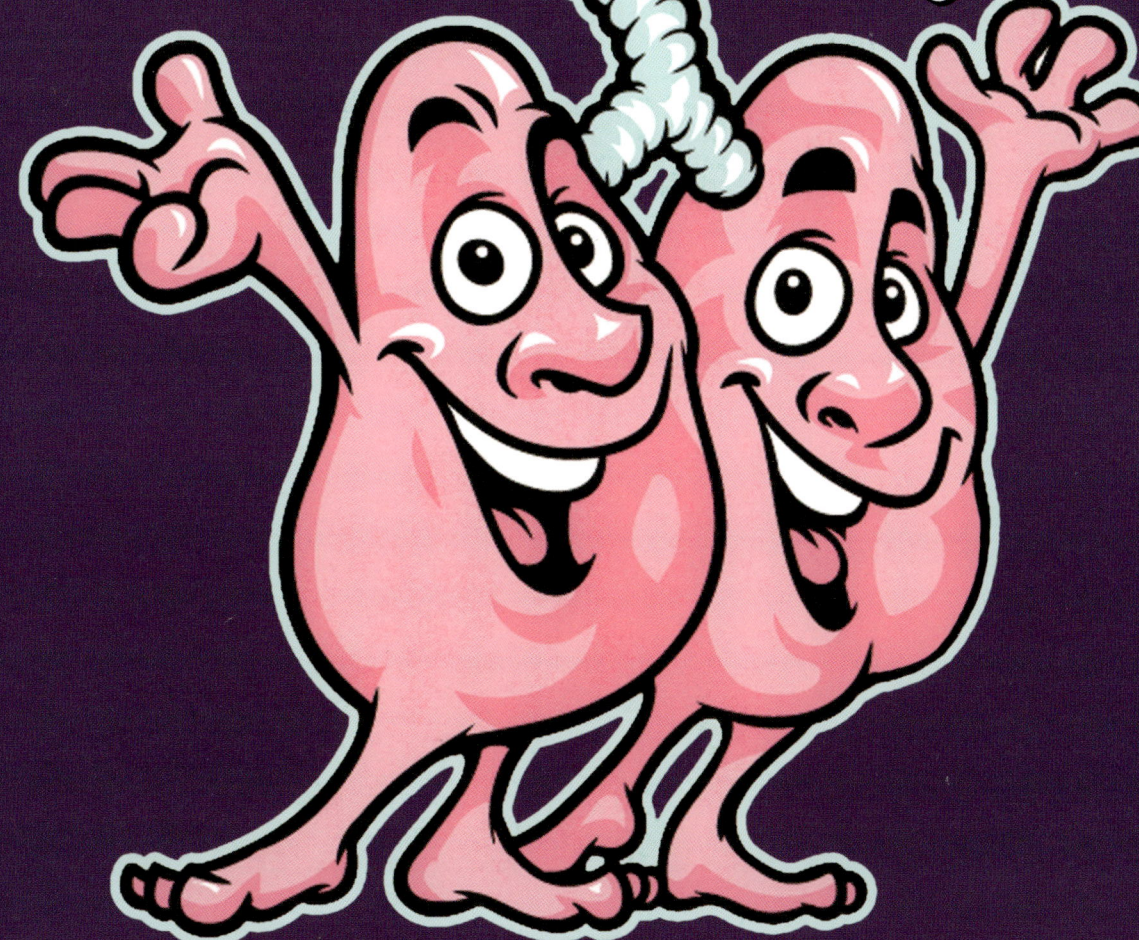

CRABTREE Publishing Company
www.crabtreebooks.com

# Crabtree Publishing Company
www.crabtreebooks.com

**Series Development, Writing, and Packaging:**
John Burstein Slim Goodbody Corp.

**Medical Reviewer:**
Christine S. Burstein, RN, MSN, FNP

**Designer:** Tammy West, Westgraphix

**Project coordinator:** Robert Walker

**Editors:** Mark Sachner, Water Buffalo Books
Molly Aloian

**Proofreader:** Adrianna Morganelli

**Production coordinator:** Katherine Berti

**Prepress technicians:** Rosie Gowsell,
Katherine Berti, Ken Wright

**Picture credits:**
© istockphoto: cover, p. 9b, 22a, 23a 27
© Shutterstock: p. 24, 25a
© Slim Goodbody: p. 7, 9a, 11a, 11b, 13a,
13b, 15, 17, 20, 21, 22b, 23b, 25b, 26

**Huff and Puff Character
Design and Illustration:**
Mike Ray, Ink Tycoon

**Medical Illustrations:** Colette Sands,
Render Ranch, and Mike Ray

"Slim Goodbody," "Huff and Puff,"
and Render Ranch illustrations,
copyright © Slim Goodbody

---

**Library and Archives Canada Cataloguing in Publication**

Burstein, John
    The remarkable respiratory system : how do my lungs
work? / John Burstein.

(Slim Goodbody's body buddies)
Includes index.
ISBN 978-0-7787-4416-0 (bound).--ISBN 978-0-7787-4430-6 (pbk.)

    1. Respiratory organs--Juvenile literature.  2. Respiration--Juvenile
literature.  I. Title.  II. Series: Burstein, John . Slim Goodbody's body
buddies.

QP121.B87 2009             j612.2            C2008-907895-0

**Library of Congress Cataloging-in-Publication Data**

Burstein, John.
   The remarkable respiratory system : how do my lungs work? /
John Burstein.
      p. cm. --  (Slim Goodbody's body buddies)
   Includes index.
   ISBN 978-0-7787-4430-6 (pbk. : alk. paper) -- ISBN 978-0-7787-4416-0
(reinforced library binding : alk. paper)
  1.  Respiration--Juvenile literature. 2.  Lungs--Juvenile literature.
I. Title. II. Series.

QP121.B94 2009
612.2--dc22
                                                          2008052416

---

## Crabtree Publishing Company
www.crabtreebooks.com        1-800-387-7650
Copyright © **2009 CRABTREE PUBLISHING COMPANY.** All rights reserved. No part of this publication may be reproduced, stored in a retrieval system or be transmitted in any form or by any means, electronic, mechanical, photocopying, recording, or otherwise, without the prior written permission of Crabtree Publishing Company.

**Published in Canada**
Crabtree Publishing
616 Welland Ave.
St. Catharines, Ontario
L2M 5V6

**Published in the United States**
Crabtree Publishing
PMB16A
350 Fifth Ave., Suite 3308
New York, NY 10118

**Published in the United Kingdom**
Crabtree Publishing
White Cross Mills
High Town, Lancaster
LA1 4XS

**Published in Australia**
Crabtree Publishing
386 Mt. Alexander Rd.
Ascot Vale (Melbourne)
VIC 3032

---

### About the Author
John Burstein (also known as Slim Goodbody) has been entertaining and educating children for over thirty years. His programs have been broadcast on CBS, PBS, Nickelodeon, USA, and Discovery. He has won numerous awards including the Parent's Choice Award and the President's Council's Fitness Leader Award. Currently, Mr. Burstein tours the country with his multimedia live show "Bodyology." For more information, please visit **slimgoodbody.com**.

# CONTENTS

MEET THE BODY BUDDIES . . . . . . . . . . . . . . . . . . . . . 4
WELCOME TO OUR WORLD . . . . . . . . . . . . . . . . . . . 6
OUR ENVELOPE OF AIR . . . . . . . . . . . . . . . . . . . . . . 8
THE STORY BEGINS . . . . . . . . . . . . . . . . . . . . . . . . . 10
A LITTLE RIDDLE . . . . . . . . . . . . . . . . . . . . . . . . . . . 12
A TREE IN ME . . . . . . . . . . . . . . . . . . . . . . . . . . . . . 14
MUSCLE MIGHT . . . . . . . . . . . . . . . . . . . . . . . . . . . 16
THE RESPIRATORY SYSTEM . . . . . . . . . . . . . . . . . . . 18
DEEP DOWN . . . . . . . . . . . . . . . . . . . . . . . . . . . . . 20
DO NOT SMOKE . . . . . . . . . . . . . . . . . . . . . . . . . . . 22
TROUBLE BELOW . . . . . . . . . . . . . . . . . . . . . . . . . . 24
MORE TROUBLE . . . . . . . . . . . . . . . . . . . . . . . . . . . 26
FABULOUS PHRASES . . . . . . . . . . . . . . . . . . . . . . . 28
AMAZING FACTS ABOUT YOUR RESPIRATORY SYSTEM . . 29
GLOSSARY . . . . . . . . . . . . . . . . . . . . . . . . . . . . . . 30
FOR MORE INFORMATION . . . . . . . . . . . . . . . . . . . . 31
INDEX . . . . . . . . . . . . . . . . . . . . . . . . . . . . . . . . . 32

Words in **bold** are defined in the glossary on page 30.

# Meet the Body Buddies

*HELLO. MY NAME IS SLIM GOODBODY.*

I am very happy that you are reading this book. It means that you want to learn about your body!

   I believe that the more you know about how your body works, the prouder you will feel.

   I believe that the prouder you feel, the more you will do to take care of yourself.

   I believe that the more you do to take care of yourself, the happier and healthier you will be.

To provide you with the very best information about how your body works, I have put together a team of good friends. I call them my Body Buddies, and I hope they will become your Body Buddies, too!

**Let me introduce them to you:**

- **HUFF AND PUFF** will guide you through the lungs and the respiratory system.

- **TICKER** will lead you on a journey to explore the heart and circulatory system.

- **COGNOS** will explain how the brain and nervous system work.

- **SQUIRT** will let you in on the secrets of tiny glands that do big jobs.

- **FLEX AND STRUT** will walk you through the workings of your bones and muscles.

- **GURGLE** will give you a tour of the stomach and digestive system.

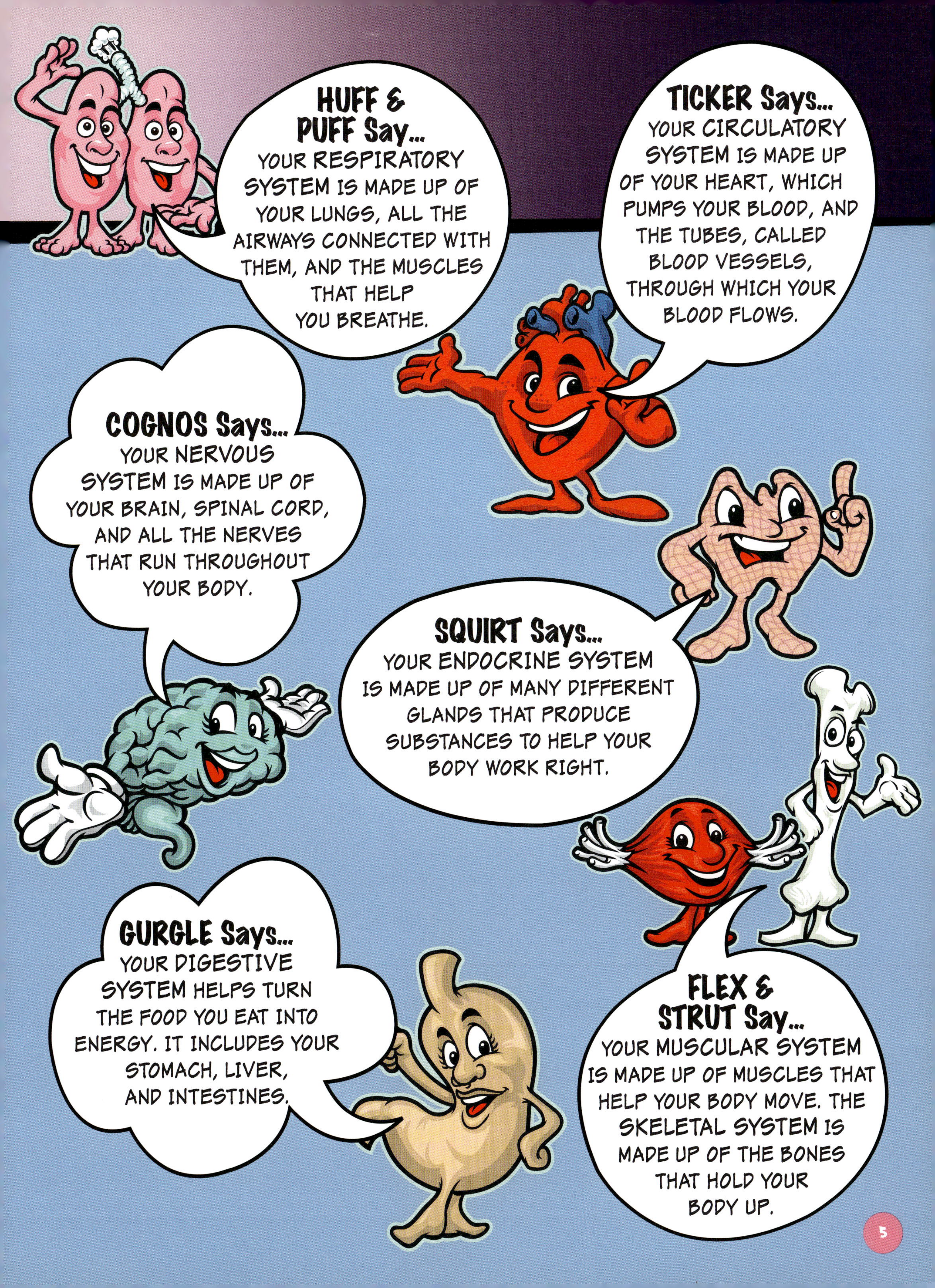

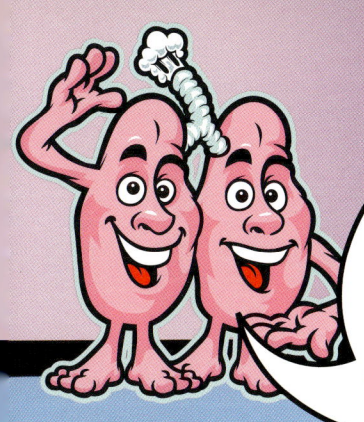

**HUFF & PUFF Say...** YOUR RESPIRATORY SYSTEM IS MADE UP OF YOUR LUNGS, ALL THE AIRWAYS CONNECTED WITH THEM, AND THE MUSCLES THAT HELP YOU BREATHE.

**TICKER Says...** YOUR CIRCULATORY SYSTEM IS MADE UP OF YOUR HEART, WHICH PUMPS YOUR BLOOD, AND THE TUBES, CALLED BLOOD VESSELS, THROUGH WHICH YOUR BLOOD FLOWS.

**COGNOS Says...** YOUR NERVOUS SYSTEM IS MADE UP OF YOUR BRAIN, SPINAL CORD, AND ALL THE NERVES THAT RUN THROUGHOUT YOUR BODY.

**SQUIRT Says...** YOUR ENDOCRINE SYSTEM IS MADE UP OF MANY DIFFERENT GLANDS THAT PRODUCE SUBSTANCES TO HELP YOUR BODY WORK RIGHT.

**GURGLE Says...** YOUR DIGESTIVE SYSTEM HELPS TURN THE FOOD YOU EAT INTO ENERGY. IT INCLUDES YOUR STOMACH, LIVER, AND INTESTINES.

**FLEX & STRUT Say...** YOUR MUSCULAR SYSTEM IS MADE UP OF MUSCLES THAT HELP YOUR BODY MOVE. THE SKELETAL SYSTEM IS MADE UP OF THE BONES THAT HOLD YOUR BODY UP.

# Welcome to Our World

**HELLO.**

MY NAME IS HUFF.

MY NAME IS PUFF.

WE ARE THE LUNG TWINS.

WE FILL WITH AIR, AND WE LET IT OUT.

BREATHING IN IS CALLED INHALING.

BREATHING OUT IS CALLED EXHALING.

NIGHT AND DAY, WE INHALE AND EXHALE, INHALE AND EXHALE, INHALE AND EXHALE.

## A Comfortable Cage

Your lungs are located inside a bony space called the rib cage. The rib cage is made up of 12 sets of ribs. Ribs are strong and hard. They protect your lungs from getting hurt.

**COGNOS says...** THE LUNGS FILL UP MOST OF THE SPACE IN THE **RIB CAGE**, BUT THERE IS STILL PLENTY OF ROOM FOR YOUR HEART.

## A LOT OF LOBES

Your lungs are made up of different sections called **lobes**. The right lung has three lobes. The left lung has only two lobes. The reason the numbers are different is that your two lungs are not the same size. The right lung is a little bigger than the left lung. This extra space on the left leaves room inside your rib cage for your heart.

right superior lobe

left superior lobe

right middle lobe

right inferior lobe

left inferior lobe

## CHEST TEST

You may not be able to see your lungs, but you can feel them working! Place your hands on your chest and breathe in deeply. You will feel your chest getting bigger and wider. Then breathe out. You can feel your chest getting smaller. You have just felt your lungs in action!

7

# Our Envelope of Air

HUMAN BEINGS LIVE IN AN ENVELOPE.

IT IS NOT THE KIND OF ENVELOPE YOU USE FOR A LETTER.

IT IS AN ENVELOPE OF AIR THAT SURROUNDS EARTH.

THIS ENVELOPE OF AIR IS CALLED THE ATMOSPHERE.

IT IS MADE UP OF MANY GASES. ONE OF THEM IS OXYGEN.

EVERY CELL IN THE BODY NEEDS OXYGEN TO LIVE.

WITH EVERY BREATH WE TAKE, WE BREATHE IN THIS LIFE-GIVING GAS.

## Cells—Our Own Energy Factories

Cells are like tiny factories. They turn food into **energy**. Cells could not do this without a steady supply of oxygen. When your cells make energy, they also make a waste product. This waste product is a gas called carbon dioxide. Carbon dioxide is what you breathe out.

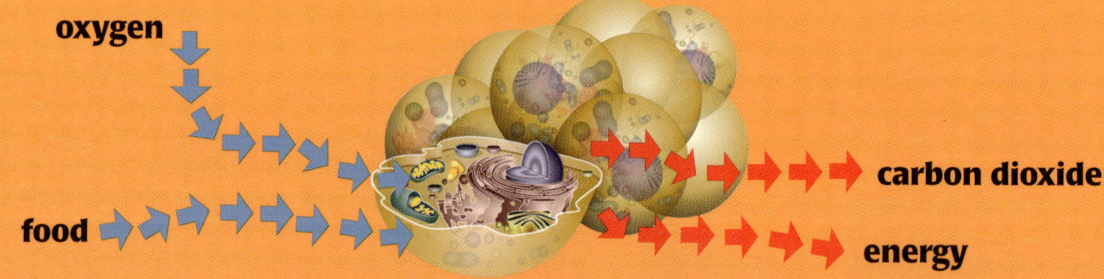

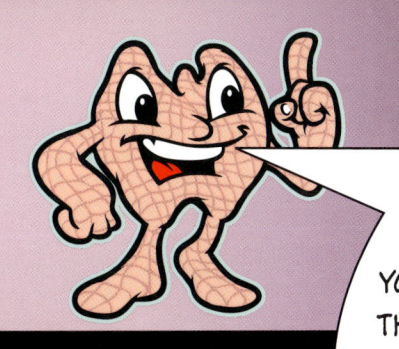

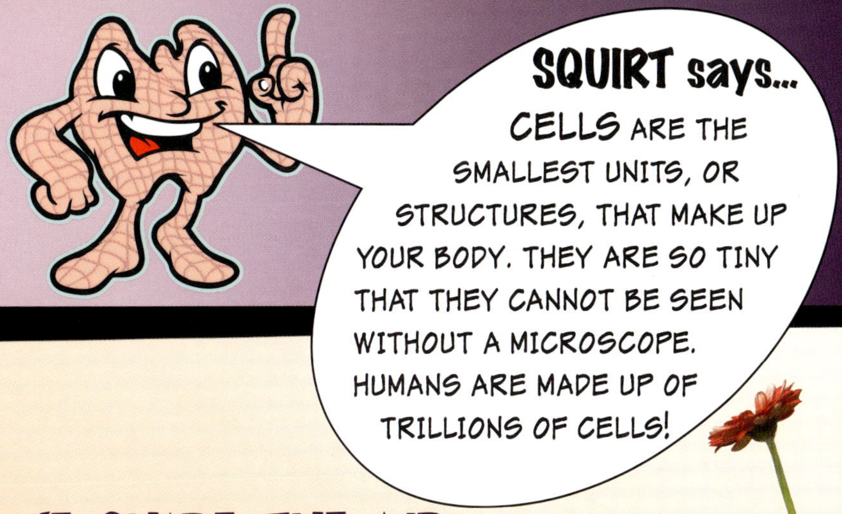

**SQUIRT says...** CELLS ARE THE SMALLEST UNITS, OR STRUCTURES, THAT MAKE UP YOUR BODY. THEY ARE SO TINY THAT THEY CANNOT BE SEEN WITHOUT A MICROSCOPE. HUMANS ARE MADE UP OF TRILLIONS OF CELLS!

## WE SHARE THE AIR

Trees, flowers, and other plants take in carbon dioxide and release oxygen. Animals breathe in oxygen and breathe out carbon dioxide. Plants and animals need each other to survive.

## BE A SCIENTIST

Here is an experiment to help you see how oxygen is needed to make energy. Be sure to get help from your parents or teacher.

**Here is what you will need:**
- A short candle
- A match
- A glass

**Directions:**

1. Light the candle.
2. Place the glass over it and see what happens.

After a few moments, the flame will go out. It goes out because the flame has used up the supply of oxygen under the glass. The flame needs oxygen to make energy, but the glass has cut off the supply of new oxygen. Without oxygen, the candle cannot make energy. The glass now contains carbon dioxide and other gases left over when oxygen is used up.

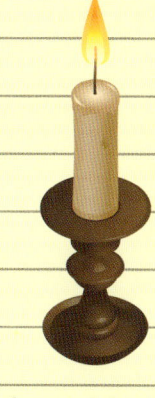

# The Story Begins

AIR MUST REACH US FIRST BEFORE WE CAN SEND IT OFF TO THE CELLS.

SOMETIMES THE AIR FLOWS IN THROUGH THE NOSE.

SOMETIMES THE AIR FLOWS IN THROUGH THE MOUTH.

NO MATTER HOW AIR ENTERS, WE ARE READY FOR IT!

## Come on in!

When you breathe in through your nostrils, the air enters tubes called the **nasal passages**. The nasal passages lead to a space called the **nasal cavity**. Behind your nasal cavity is a passageway called the pharynx. Whether you breathe in through your nose or your mouth, the air flows into the pharynx before heading down to your lungs.

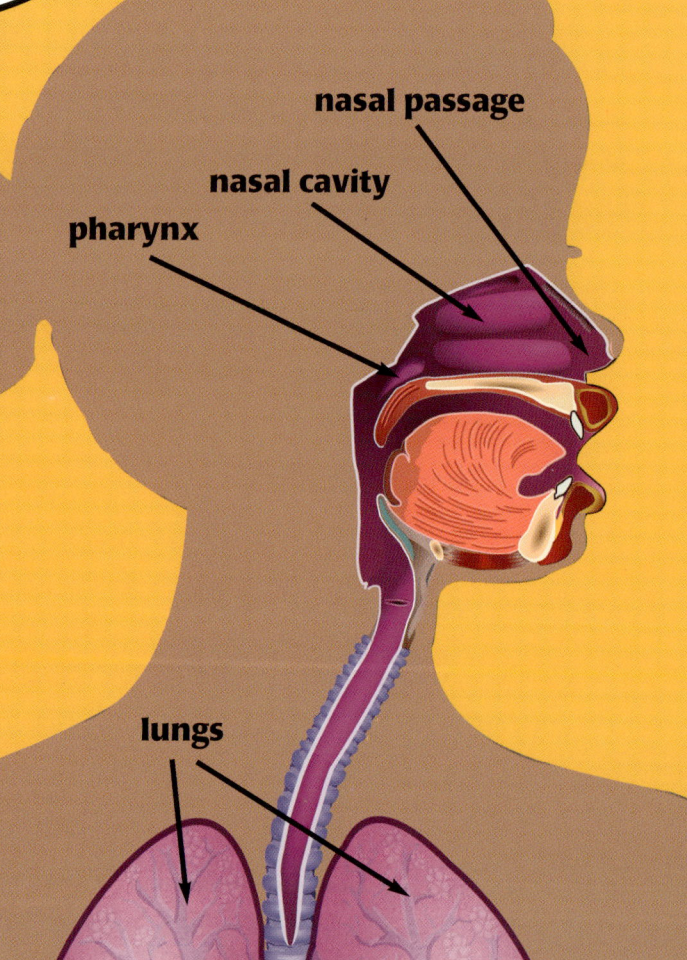

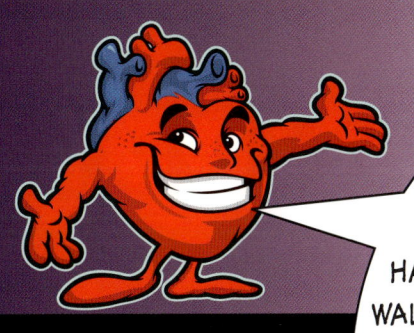

**TICKER says...** THE NASAL PASSAGES ARE SEPARATED BY A WALL CALLED THE **SEPTUM**. YOUR HEART ALSO HAS A SEPTUM. IT IS THE THICK WALL THAT RUNS DOWN THE CENTER OF THE HEART. THE SEPTUM SEPARATES THE LEFT SIDE AND THE RIGHT SIDE OF THE HEART.

## THE NOSE KNOWS

Breathing in through your nose is often healthier than breathing in through your mouth. Your nose warms and cleans the air. The inside of your nose is lined with a thin sticky layer of mucus. Mucus traps **germs**, dust, and other small particles before they reach your lungs. When you blow your nose, the problem particles are ejected.

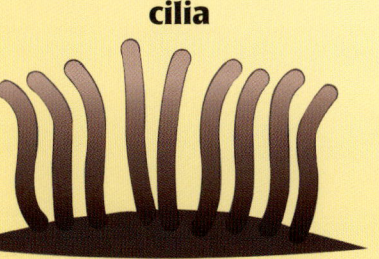

cilia

## SWEEP IT UP

There are also tiny hairs in your nose called cilia. Cilia help catch and remove larger particles such as dirt and pollen that do not get trapped in the mucus. As you breathe in, the cilia move back and forth. They sweep the particles up and away from your lungs.

## WHAT A BLAST!

When you sneeze, you send air flying out of your nose at about 100 miles (160 km) per hour! If your sneeze was a car, it would get a speeding ticket!

# A LITTLE RIDDLE

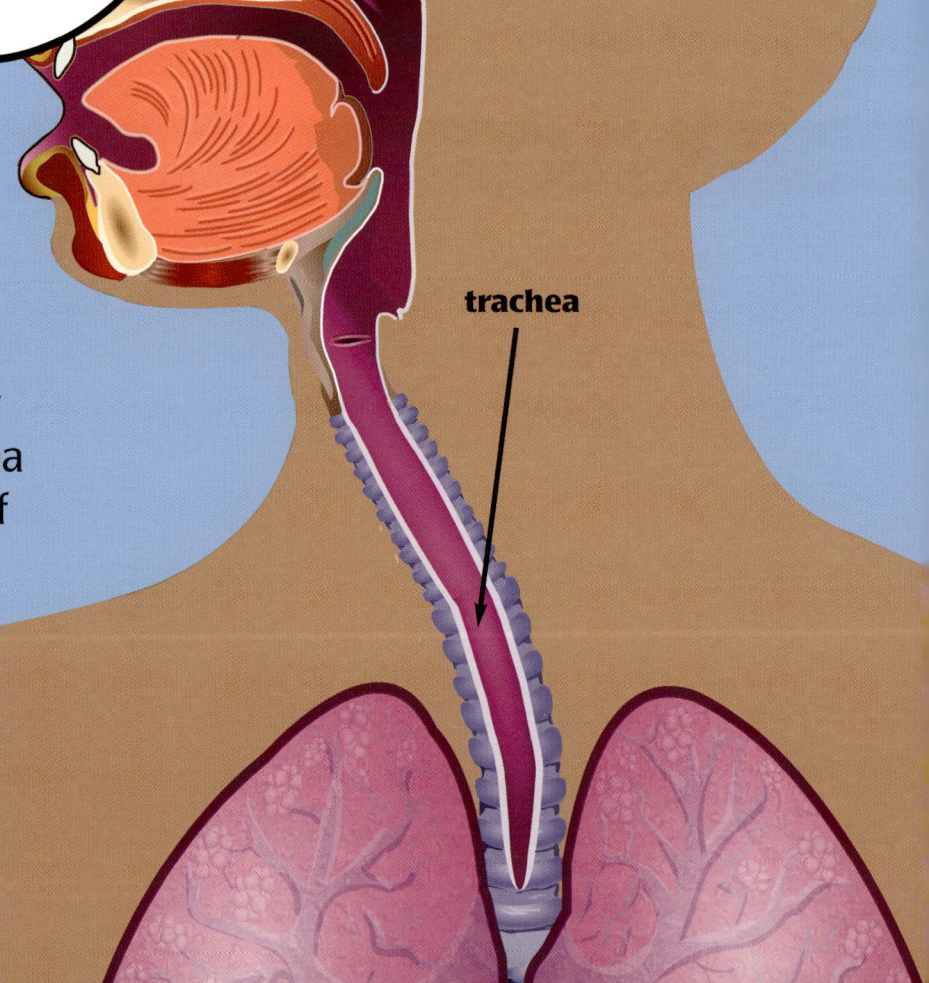

WE WROTE A POEM. IT IS A BIT OF A RIDDLE.
FIGURE OUT THE ANSWER IF YOU CAN:

ONCE AIR PASSES NOSE OR MOUTH
IT TAKES A TURN AND THEN HEADS SOUTH.

HERE'S A QUESTION JUST FOR YOU:
WHAT TUBE IS IT THAT AIR FLOWS THROUGH?

## PIPE DOWN!

The answer is the windpipe, or trachea. The air flows through your trachea on its way to the lungs. The trachea runs down the center of the front part of your neck. It is 3.9 to 4.7 inches (10–12 cm) long and a little more than half an inch (1.3 cm) in diameter.

**GURGLE says...** A SPECIAL FLAP OF SKIN CALLED THE **EPIGLOTTIS** COVERS THE TOP OF YOUR TRACHEA. WHEN YOU EAT OR DRINK, THE EPIGLOTTIS FLAPS DOWN AND CLOSES OVER YOUR TRACHEA TO MAKE SURE NO FOOD GETS INTO YOUR LUNGS.

# SPEAK UP!

At the top of the trachea is the voice box, or larynx. Across the top of the larynx are two bands of stretchy material called vocal cords. When you breathe out, the air moves up the trachea and flows past the vocal cords. The moving air makes the vocal cords vibrate back and forth. As the vocal cords vibrate, they make sound. That sound is what you hear when you speak or sing. It is the sound of your voice!

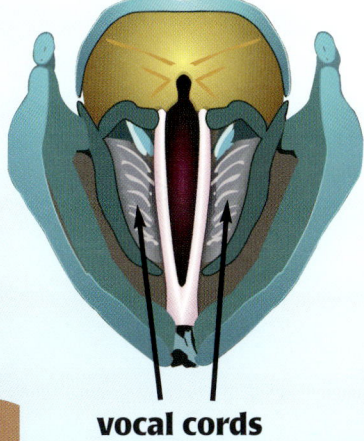

# BE A SCIENTIST

Your trachea is strong, but it is not rigid. It is something like a vacuum hose. Your trachea is flexible enough to let you breathe and move at the same time. Try this experiment to find your trachea and prove how flexible it is.

**Here is what you will need:**
- Your head
- Your neck
- Your hand

### Directions:
1. Rub your hand up and down on the front of your neck.
2. Shake your head "no" while you breathe in.
3. Nod your head "yes" while you breathe out.

When you rub your hand on your neck, you will feel something bumpy. You have found your trachea! You have also shown that your flexible trachea allows you to move your head and breathe at the same time.

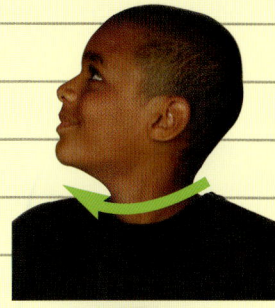
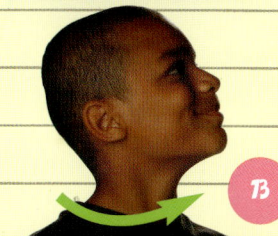

# A Tree in Me

YOU HAVE AN UPSIDE DOWN TREE IN YOUR BODY.

IT IS CALLED THE **BRONCHIAL** TREE.

THE TRACHEA IS THE TRUNK OF THE BRONCHIAL TREE.

THERE ARE A LOT OF BRANCHES THAT SPREAD OUT FROM THE TRACHEA.

READ ON AND FIND OUT ALL ABOUT IT.

## THE BRONCHIAL TREE

The trachea divides into two big branches called the bronchial tubes, or bronchi. Each branch, called a bronchus, enters a lung. Each bronchus keeps dividing into smaller and smaller branches, called bronchioles. At the end of the bronchioles are clusters of teeny tiny air sacs called alveoli.

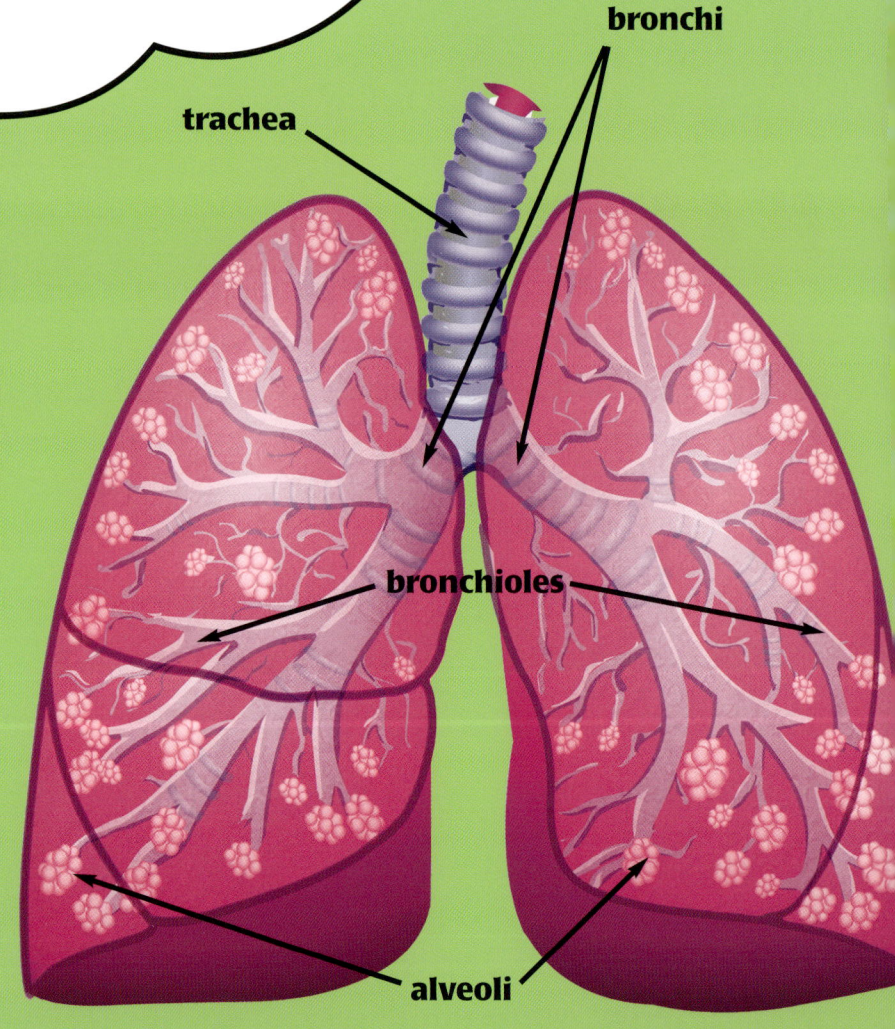

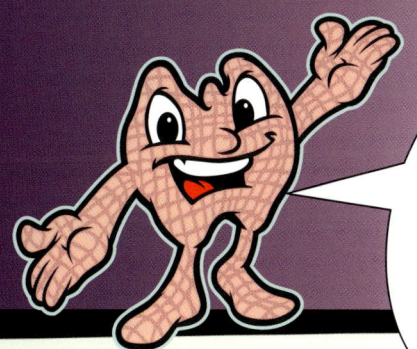

SQUIRT says... ALVEOLI ARE LIKE LEAVES ON YOUR UPSIDE DOWN BRONCHIAL TREE. YOUR BRONCHI HAVE ABOUT 600 MILLION ALVEOLI IN ALL!

## ALL ABOUT ALVEOLI

Alveoli have very thin walls. The oxygen you breathe in slips through these walls into tiny blood vessels called capillaries. The blood moving through the capillaries picks up the oxygen and carries it to the cells of your body. When you breathe out, the process happens in reverse. Carbon dioxide flows through the capillaries into the alveoli. Then the carbon dioxide moves up through the bronchioles, into the bronchi, the trachea, and out into the air.

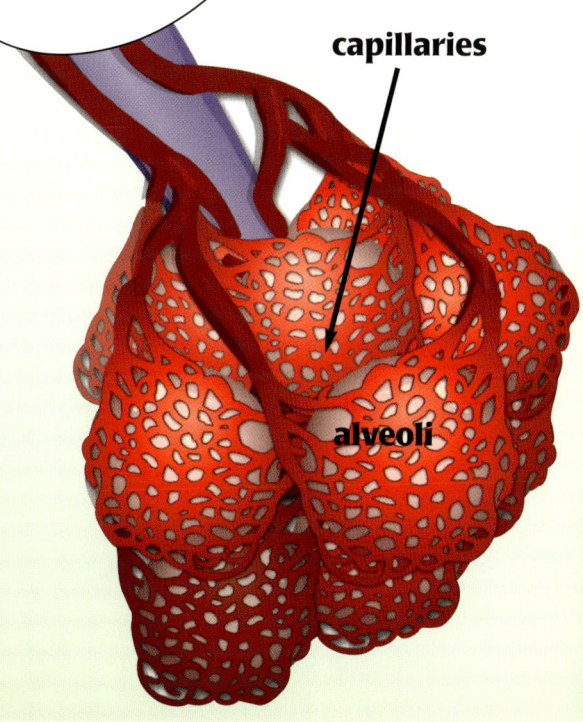

## BE A SCIENTIST

The air that you exhale has been warmed up in your body. Try this experiment to demonstrate the difference between the temperature of the air outside and inside your body.

Here is what you will need:
- Your mouth and nose
- Your hand

### Directions:

1. Take a big breath in through your nose.
2. Put your hand a few inches in front of your mouth.
3. Breathe out through your mouth onto your hand.

When you breathe out, how does the air feel? Is it warmer than the air around you?

# Muscle Might

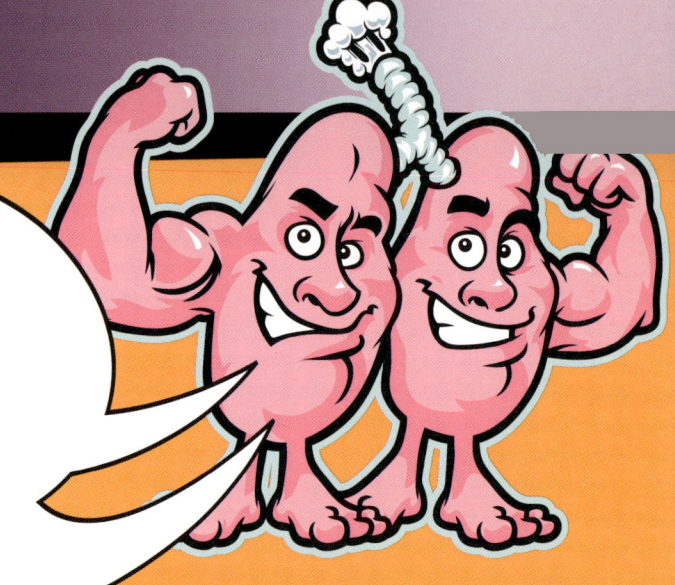

WE CANNOT MOVE AIR IN AND OUT ALL BY OURSELVES.

WE MUST RELY ON MUSCLES TO HELP US DO OUR JOB.

WE DEPEND UPON A BIG MUSCLE LOCATED BELOW US.

WE DEPEND ON OTHER SMALLER MUSCLES THAT SURROUND US.

## A Living Room

Between your ribs are intercostal muscles. Intercostal muscles move your ribs so they can expand and contract. Below your lungs is a large, dome-shaped muscle called the diaphragm. The diaphragm can move up and down. When your diaphragm moves down and your ribs expand, air flows into your lungs. When your diaphragm moves up and your ribs contract, air is pushed out of your lungs.

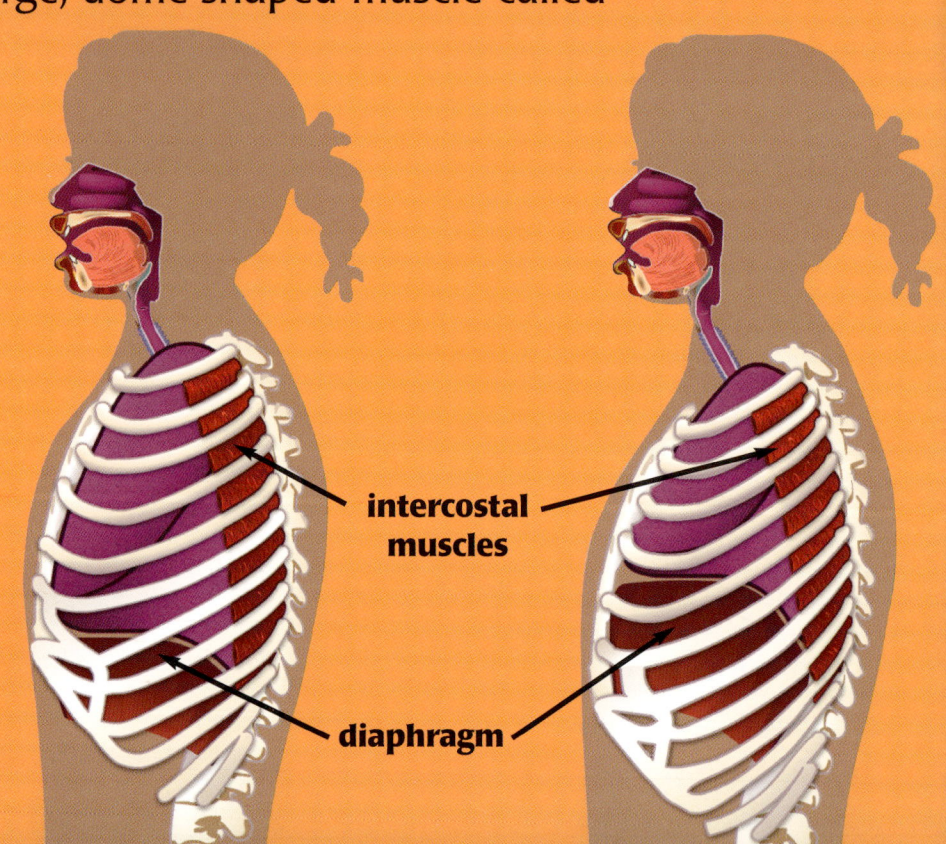

*FLEX & STRUT say...* THE RIB CAGE IS MADE UP OF 12 SETS OF RIBS, THE BREASTBONE, OR STERNUM, AND THE UPPER BONES OF YOUR SPINE.

## IT ALL ADDS UP!

As people grow older and their lungs get bigger, their breathing slows. The number of breaths they take gets lower. Here are some average breathing rates:
- Newborns: 40–50 breaths per minute
- Infants: 20–40 breaths per minute
- Preschool children: 20–30 breaths per minute
- Older children: 16–25 breaths per minute
- Adults: 12–20 breaths per minute

## BE A SCIENTIST

Try this experiment to figure out how many times you breathe in an hour, a day, a week, and a year.

**Here is what you will need:**
- A calculator
- A piece of paper
- A pencil or pen

### Directions:

1. Write down the number "20" on the piece of paper. We will use this as an average number of breaths most kids take in a minute. Write down all your answers on the paper as you go along.
2. Multiply that number by 60. This is the number of breaths you take each hour.
3. Multiply that number by 24. This is how many breaths you take each day.
4. Multiply that number by 7. This is how many breaths you take each week.
5. Multiply that number by 52. This is how many breaths you take in a year.

Think how many breaths you will take by the time you are 70!

# The Respiratory System

- nasal passages
- nasal cavity
- pharynx
- trachea

18

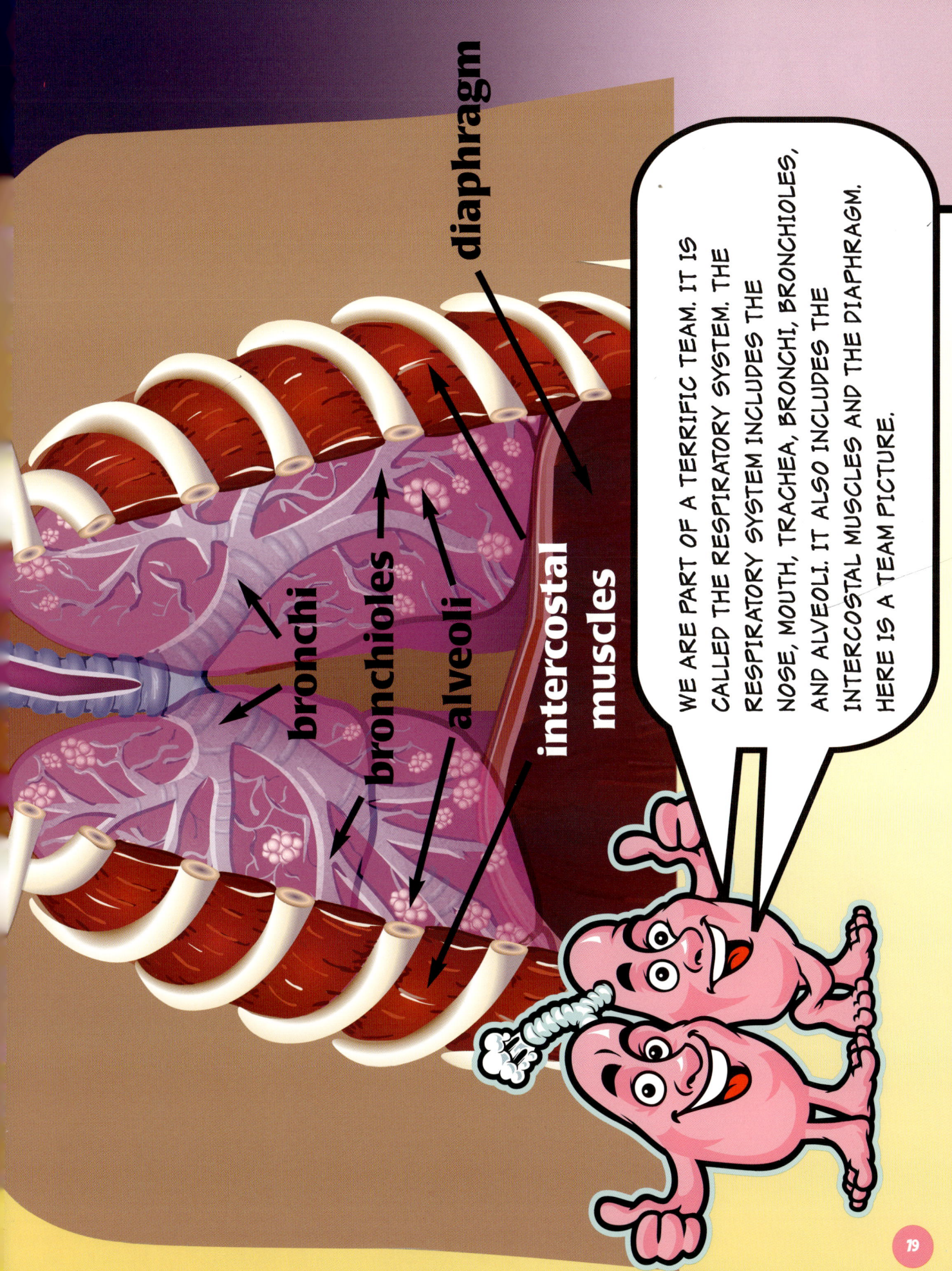

# Deep Down

> WE LIKE TO FEEL FULL FROM BOTTOM TO TOP.
>
> WE CAN HOLD A LOT MORE AIR THAN MOST PEOPLE THINK WE CAN.
>
> BREATHING DEEPLY AND SLOWLY IS THE BEST WAY TO FILL US UP.
>
> OUR JOB IS TO HELP GET A LOT OF OXYGEN TO THE CELLS.
>
> WHEN WE HAVE MORE OXYGEN TO WORK WITH, WE DO OUR JOB BETTER.

## Half Full

Most people do not breathe deeply enough. They take **shallow breaths** that fill less than half the amount of lung space available.

## Dump the Slump

Practice good posture. When you stand or sit, do not slump. If you hunch over, your chest gets cramped and your lungs have a harder time filling with air. When you sit and stand up straight, your lungs have the room they need to expand.

FLEX & STRUT say... THE POSITION OF YOUR BODY WHEN YOU ARE SITTING OR STANDING IS CALLED YOUR POSTURE. HAVING GOOD POSTURE HELPS YOUR LUNGS BREATHE MORE EASILY.

## BETTER BREATHING

You can improve your breathing by learning to take slow, deep breaths. Here are two ways to practice:

1. Place your hands on your chest. Inhale slowly as you silently count to four. Feel your chest expand as your lungs fill with air. Hold your breath for a count of four. Exhale slowly to a count of six. Repeat this pattern ten times in a row. Practice once a day for a week.

   In the second week, slow your breathing down. Inhale to a count of five. Hold for a count of five. Exhale to a count of eight. Repeat this pattern 12 times in a row. Practice once a day for a week.

   Week after week increase the time you inhale, hold, and exhale. You will soon be in the habit of breathing more deeply.

2. Take a deep breath and count the number of times you can say, "I love my lovely lungs" out loud before you run out of air. Practice every day for a month and see if the number increases.

# Do Not Smoke

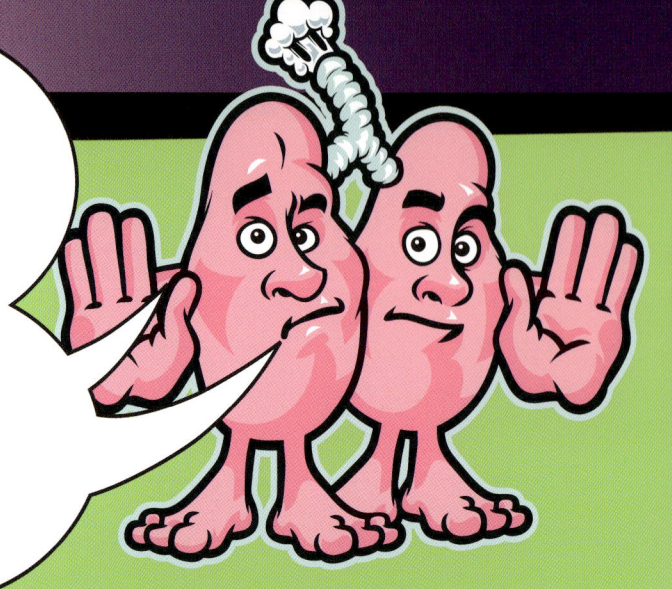

"THERE IS NOTHING WE HATE MORE THAN SMOKING. WE HATE, HATE, HATE, HATE IT! IT IS STINKY AND DISGUSTING. IT IS HORRIBLE AND FILTHY. IT IS REALLY, REALLY BAD FOR US — AND FOR YOU!"

## IT MAKES NO SENSE

It makes no sense to smoke. Here are a few reasons why:

1. Cigarette smoke breaks the thin walls of your alveoli. When alveoli are destroyed, you get less oxygen into your blood.

2. Smoking can cause a disease called cancer.

3. Cigarette smokers have more than twice the risk of a heart attack as people who do not smoke.

4. Smoking can shorten your life by ten years or more.

5. Smoking stains your teeth yellow and makes your mouth smell bad.

6. Smokers get more colds, **flu**, **bronchitis**, **pneumonia** and other diseases than people who do not smoke.

**COGNOS says...** CHEMICALS IN CIGARETTE SMOKE CAN MAKE YOU SICK IN SO MANY WAYS! THEY PUT POISONS INTO YOUR BLOOD AND CAN WEAKEN YOUR HEART. THEY MAKE IT HARDER TO FIGHT MANY DISEASES, INCLUDING CANCER—AND ESPECIALLY LUNG CANCER.

## CAN YOU BELIEVE IT?

Cigarette smoke contains almost five thousand chemicals! Many of these chemicals are poisonous. Here are a few:

- **Arsenic:** found in rat poison
- **Methane:** found in rocket fuel
- **Carbon Monoxide:** found in car **exhaust**
- **Ammonia:** found in floor cleaners
- **Cadmium:** found in batteries
- **Butane:** found in lighter fluid

When someone inhales cigarette smoke, small amounts of these chemicals get into their blood. Then the chemicals travel to all the parts of the body and cause harm.

## SECONDHAND SMOKE

Even if you do not smoke, you are at risk just by standing close to someone who does. This kind of smoke, called secondhand smoke, comes from two sources:

1. Smoke exhaled by someone who is smoking.
2. Smoke coming from a lit cigarette, cigar, or pipe.

Walk away from nearby smokers. If you know them, ask them to smoke outside.

# TROUBLE BELOW

> THE BRONCHIAL TREE LETS IN AIR.
>
> IT ALSO LETS IN GERMS.
>
> A LOT OF THE GERMS GET TRAPPED BEFORE THEY REACH US.
>
> BUT A LOT OF THE GERMS STILL GET THROUGH!
>
> THIS CAN CAUSE TROUBLE FOR THE BODY.
>
> WE DO OUR BEST, BUT SOMETIMES WE GET SICK.

## SICK LIST

If germs get into your respiratory system, they can make you sick. Here are a few of the respiratory illnesses caused by germs:

1. Colds
2. Flu
3. Pneumonia
4. Whooping cough
5. Bronchitis

24

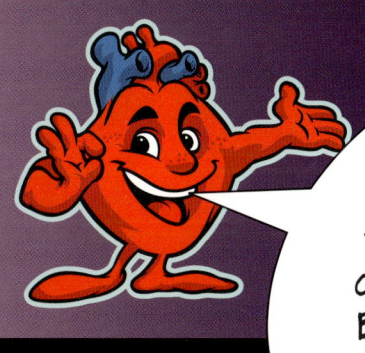

**TICKER says...**
THE BLOOD I PUMP THROUGH THE BODY CONTAINS **WHITE BLOOD CELLS**. WHITE BLOOD CELLS FIGHT GERMS.

## ALL WASHED UP

Believe it or not, most germs get carried into your body by your hands! That is why it is so important to wash your hands before you eat and after you go to the bathroom. Washing kills these germs before they can start trouble. To do a good job, use soap and warm water. Keep washing for about 15–20 seconds—or about as long as it takes to sing the "Happy Birthday" song twice.

## SLEEPY TIME

To stay healthy, it is important to get enough sleep every night. Give your lungs a treat while you sleep! Make sure there is plenty of fresh air in your bedroom.

# More Trouble

> GERMS DO NOT CAUSE ALL OF OUR TROUBLES.
>
> AIR POLLUTION IS ALSO A PROBLEM.
>
> DIRT AND DUST IN THE AIR ARE NOT GOOD FOR US.
>
> WE LOVE CLEAN AIR, BUT BREATHING IS OUR JOB ... AND WE CANNOT HELP BREATHING IN WHAT IS OUTSIDE.

## Ahchoo!

Allergies are not caused by germs. You might be **allergic** to plants, flowers, dust, peanuts, milk, pets, or antibiotics. If you come close to something you are allergic to, here is what can happen:

- Your nose may run and you may start sneezing.
- You might find it hard to breathe.
- Your eyes may tear and feel itchy.

Some medicines might help you feel better, but they do not cure allergies. The best thing to do is stay away from things that cause the allergy.

**COGNOS says...** NOBODY KNOWS FOR CERTAIN WHY PEOPLE HAVE ALLERGIES. FOR UNKNOWN REASONS WHAT IS HARMLESS TO SOME PEOPLE CAN CAUSE PROBLEMS FOR OTHERS.

## ASTHMA

Asthma is the number-one reason that kids miss school. Asthma is not caused by germs. It is not a disease that is cured in a week, a month, or even a year. If you have asthma, it may last your whole life. When a person with asthma breathes in cigarette smoke, dust, or pet **dander**, it can set off an asthma attack. When someone has an asthma attack, here is what happens:

- The airways in the lungs become narrower and get clogged with mucus.
- It becomes harder to breathe, and it can hurt to try.
- It can cause sharp chest pains and coughing.

One way of treating asthma is to take special medicine to open up the airways in the lungs. Most people use an inhaler to breathe this medicine right into their lungs.

# FABULOUS PHRASES

BEFORE WE LEAVE YOU, WE WANT TO PLAY A GAME. IN THE BOX BELOW YOU WILL SEE EIGHT PHRASES. EACH PHRASE HAS THE WORD "BREATH" IN IT.

WE WILL START A SENTENCE AND YOU TRY TO FILL IN THE BLANK USING ONE OF THE PHRASES.

FOR EXAMPLE, IF THE SENTENCE NUMBER 1 IS: THE SUNSET WAS SO BEAUTIFUL, IT _____ .

YOU WOULD CHOOSE THE PHRASE "A": "TOOK MY BREATH AWAY." GOT IT?

Remember, choose a phrase that completes the sentence. The right matches of sentences and phrases are at the bottom of the page. But you will have to turn the book upside down to read them!

1. The sunset was so beautiful, it _____ .
2. If someone will not listen to you, why _____ ?
3. If you have just run a race you may need to _____ .
4. If it is stuffy in a room, you may want to go outside for a _____ .
5. If you are upset, you might mutter something _____ .
6. If there is no use in asking for something, you might as well _____ .
7. If you missed the bus and had to jog to school you might be really _____ .

| A. took my breath away | B. out of breath | C. save your breath |
| D. waste your breath | E. under your breath | F. breath of fresh air |
| G. catch your breath | | |

ANSWERS: 1A, 2D, 3G, 4F, 5E, 6C, 7B

# Amazing Facts About Your Respiratory System

YOUR LUNGS CONTAIN ALMOST 1,500 MILES (2,414 KM) OF AIRWAYS.

BRONCHIOLES ARE ABOUT THE SAME THICKNESS AS HAIR.

A SINGLE CIGARETTE CAN TAKE ABOUT FIVE TO 20 MINUTES OFF A PERSON'S LIFE.

THERE ARE ABOUT 600 MILLION ALVEOLI IN YOUR LUNGS, AND IF YOU STRETCHED THEM OUT, THEY WOULD COVER AN ENTIRE TENNIS COURT.

SMOKERS GET THREE TIMES MORE CAVITIES THAN NON-SMOKERS.

YAWNING BRINGS EXTRA OXYGEN INTO THE LUNGS. YAWNING ALSO GETS RID OF CARBON DIOXIDE THAT MAY BE BUILDING UP IN THE LUNGS.

AN ORDINARY GROWN-UP TAKES ABOUT 16 BREATHS IN ONE MINUTE WHEN AWAKE. DURING SLEEP, THAT RATE MAY LOWER TO SIX TO EIGHT BREATHS.

MILLIONS OF TINY HAIRS CALLED CILIA WORK IN YOUR TRACHEA AND NOSE LIKE TINY BROOMS TO SWEEP OUT DIRT AND DUST FROM YOUR LUNGS EACH ONE OF THE CILIA SWEEPS BACK AND FORTH ABOUT TEN TIMES EVERY SECOND!

CHILDREN AND WOMEN BREATHE FASTER THAN MEN.

# Glossary

**allergic** Having a reaction to certain substances, such as dust, plants, some foods, or animal fur leading to sneezing, runny eyes and nose, or difficulty breathing

**bronchial** Having to do with the bronchi (bronchial tubes) that lead from the trachea (windpipe) to the lungs

**bronchitis** An illness that infects the lining of the bronchial tubes in which the tubes swell up and create a lot of mucus, sometimes leading to a bad cough to get rid of the mucus

**dander** Scaly or dry skin in an animal's fur, coat, or feathers that may cause an allergic reaction or asthma attack in humans

**energy** Power or force; a lively action using a lot of power or force

**exhaust** Smoke or fumes that come from an engine, usually through the tailpipe of a car

**flu** A severe infection of the respiratory system causing fever, body aches, and the build-up of mucus

**germs** Tiny living beings so small they cannot be seen without a microscope. Most are bacteria or viruses that can cause illness

**lobes** Parts of sections of something, either divided into segments, such as the lobes of the lungs, or hanging, like earlobes

**nasal cavity** The inside of the nose, just beyond the nasal passages

**nasal passages** The front parts of the nose leading from the nostrils toward the nasal cavity

**pneumonia** An infection of one or both lungs in which fluid builds up in the lungs and it becomes difficult to breathe deeply or catch one's breath

**shallow breaths** Short, usually fast breaths that do not deeply fill the lungs and may take more effort than deep breathing; may be caused by poor posture or nervousness

# For More Information

## Books

*How Do Your Lungs Work* (Rookie Read-About Health). Don L. Curry. Children's Press.

*Human Body.* (DK Eyewitness Books). Steve Parker. DK Children.

*The Incredible Human Body.* Esther Weiner. Scholastic Inc.

*Learning About My Body.* Jo Ellen Moore. Evan-Moor Educational Publishers. Scholastic Reference.

*Lungs: Your Respiratory System.* Seymour Simon. Collins.

*Lungs and Respiration* (Exploring the Human Body). Carol Ballard. Franklin Watts Ltd.

## Websites

**Canadian Lung Association**
www.lung.ca/lung101-renseignez/students-etudiants_e.php
Games and interactive website about the human respiratory system

**Kids Health for Kids**
kidshealth.org/kid/htbw/lungs.html
Check out this website for information on your lungs and respiratory system.

**Minneapolis Heart Foundation**
www.mplsheartfoundation.org/kids/
Visit this website for some interactive learning about your heart and a free healthy heart certificate.

**Slim Goodbody**
www.slimgoodbody.com
Discover loads of fun and free downloads for kids, teachers, and parents.

# Index

**A**ir  6, 8, 9, 10, 11, 15, 20, 21, 24, 25
   flow of  10, 12, 13, 15
   tubes  12, 18–19
air pollution  26
airways  27, 29
allergies  26, 27
alveoli  14–15, 18–19, 22, 29
asthma  27

**B**lood  5, 15, 22, 25
blood cells  5, 25
blood vessels  5
bones  4, 5, 17, 21
brain  4, 5
breathing  5, 6, 7, 8, 9, 10, 11, 13, 18–19
   deep vs. shallow  20–21
   rate of  17, 29
   trouble with  26–27
bronchi (bronchial tubes)  14–15, 18–19
bronchial tree  14–15, 24
bronchioles  15, 18–19, 29

**C**apillaries  15
carbon dioxide  8–9, 15, 29
cells  8, 9, 10, 15, 20
chest  7, 20, 21, 27

cilia  11, 29
circulation and circulatory system  4, 5

**D**iaphragm  16, 18–19
digestion and digestive system  4, 5

**E**ndocrine system  4
energy  5, 8–9
epiglottis  13
exhaling  6, 15

**G**erms  11, 24, 25, 26, 27

**H**eart  4, 7, 22, 23

**I**nhaler  27
inhaling  6, 21, 23
intercostal muscles  16

**L**arynx  13
liver  5
lobes  7
lung cancer  23
lungs  4, 6
   flow of air into and out of  12, 13, 15, 16, 21
   illness or damage to  22–23, 24–25, 27
   left vs. right  7, 14
   protection of  6, 11, 13, 15, 25, 29

mouth  10, 11, 12, 15, 18–19, 22

**M**ucus  11, 27
muscles  4, 5, 16, 18–19

**N**asal cavity  10, 18–19
nasal passages  10, 11, 18–19
nervous system  4, 5
nose  10, 11, 12, 15, 18–19, 26, 29

**O**xygen  8–9, 15, 20, 22, 29

**P**harynx  10, 18–19

**R**espiratory system  4, 18–19, 24
ribs  6, 16, 17

**S**eptum  11
skeletal system  5
smoking  22–23
sneezing  11
spinal cord  5
sternum (breastbone)  7, 17
stomach  4, 5

**T**rachea (windpipe)  12–13, 14, 15, 18–19, 29

**V**ocal cords  15

Printed in the U.S.A. - CG

612.2 B
Burstein, John.
The remarkable respiratory system
:how do my lungs work? /
TUTTLE
03/12